JUST LISTEN

To the members of my critique group—
for all the times they had to listen to this
before I got it right.
W. M.

To Cherie and Jimmy R.
P. C-C.

JUST LISTEN

by Winifred Morris

illustrated by Patricia Cullen-Clark

Macmillan/McGraw-Hill School Publishing Company

New York Chicago Columbus

Tara lived in a city with sounds all around her. Inside she could hear the hum of the refrigerator. She could hear the click and whir of the furnace. Sometimes talking and noise came from the television set. Often her little brother yelled. But even when the TV was quiet and her little brother was napping—even when her father was reading, stretched out so long on the couch that his feet poked off one end—even when her mother, too, was reading, her feet tucked under her in the overstuffed chair—even when the refrigerator was silent and it was too warm to run the furnace, Tara could hear sounds all around her.

Some of the sounds she could name. A jet overhead. A siren in the distance. Children at the park. The dog down the street. Then cars swishing past—one this way, one that way.

Another car swishing past. On the street in front of her house. On the street behind her house.

But there were so many streets—there were so many cars—that it wasn't just one swish and then another. The swishing never stopped. Not even in the middle of the night. Not even when a scary dream wakened her so that she lay in bed, listening.

Then she could hear the hum of the refrigerator very clearly, and the click and whir of the furnace—also the swishing, the endless swishing, more like a roar, really, from the city all around her.

On the third Sunday of every month, however, Tara and her family went to Grandma's house. And Grandma didn't live in the city. They had to drive for two hours, over a mountain, down along a river, then through fields of wheat that were sometimes brown, sometimes green, sometimes golden, sometimes white.

Grandma lived in a cabin that smelled of woodsmoke and fresh bread.

After dinner, Grandma would take Tara by the hand. She would lead her out into the twilight. They would walk until the cabin was far behind them. There they would stop. And just listen.

"Just listen." That was what Grandma would say.

Tara would hear the chatter of squirrels, the rustle of wind, the swoop of wings diving to catch a mouse on the run. She might then hear the call of the owl low in the distance, or the voice of a coyote slice shrill through the darkness. But when the squirrels were quiet and the wind was still, when the owls and the coyotes were listening, too, Grandma would whisper into the silence, "Now what do you hear?"

"I hear nothing. No, I hear something."
Only Tara's eyes would ask the question.
Then Grandma would tell her again. "You hear your own special song" is what she would say. "It's there all the time, but it's very, very soft. Try never to forget it, now that you've heard it."

But then Grandma moved into the city.

When Tara went to visit her, Grandma's two-room apartment on the seventh floor of a very tall building sounded just like her own home. It was full of clicks and whirs and a low, endless roar.

As Tara grew older, she grew very, very busy. She took ballet. She took karate. She played the piano. She played shortstop.

She forgot she had once heard a song in the silence, a song Grandma had told her was her own special song. For she heard no silence.

But Grandma didn't forget.

One day Grandma said, "Couldn't we go there, just for a short visit?" She said she wanted to see the little cabin again and also the wheat fields that were sometimes brown, sometimes green, sometimes golden, sometimes white.

"But it's such a long trip away," Tara's father told her.

And Tara's mother insisted, "There's nothing there anymore."

"Nothing?" said Grandma.

They had to drive for two hours, over the mountain, then down along the river. When they got to the cabin, they found it cold and dark. It smelled of dirt and dampness. Grandma stood in the kitchen and said she could still see it just the way it used to be. But Tara couldn't.

Then Grandma walked out into the twilight.
Tara followed her, laughing and talking about
school, about baseball. They walked until the
cabin was far behind them. But when they
stopped, Tara remembered.

She remembered to listen.

"Just listen." That was what Grandma said.

Tara heard a skittering in the hedgerow. She heard a fluttering in the pale sky. She heard a howl in the distance. Then quiet. And she listened to the quiet.

"It's still there," she whispered. "My song is still there."

"Yes," said Grandma. "It's always there. But you have to listen. You have to listen very closely. Now you can feel the harmony, the rhythm, the pattern of it—the beauty of it that ripples through everything you do."

Then, for a long time, the two of them just listened.

Atheneum
Macmillan Publishing Company
866 Third Avenue,
New York, NY 10022

Collier Macmillan Canada, Inc.
For information regarding permission, write to
Macmillan Publishing Company,
866 Third Avenue,
New York, NY 10022.
This edition is reprinted by arrangement with **Macmillan Publishing Company.**

Macmillan/McGraw-Hill School Division
10 Union Square East
New York, New York 10003

Printed and bound in Mexico.
ISBN 0-02-274915-2

1 2 3 4 5 6 7 8 9 REY 99 98 97 96 95 94 93 92